Purchased from
Multnomah County Library
Title Wave Used Bookstore
216 NE Knott St, Portland, OR
503-988-5021

D1441854

Arty!
The Greatest Artist in the World

williambee

STERLING CHILDREN'S BOOKS
New York

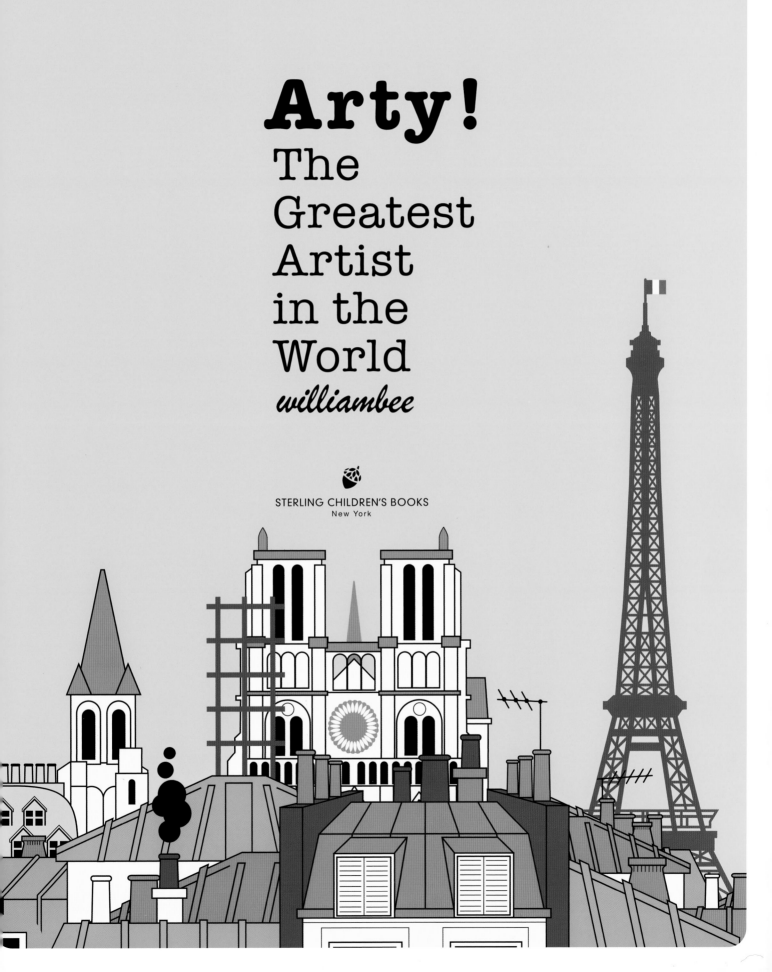

STERLING CHILDREN'S BOOKS
New York

An Imprint of Sterling Publishing Co., Inc.
1166 Avenue of the Americas
New York, NY 10036

STERLING CHILDREN'S BOOKS and the distinctive Sterling Children's Books logo are registered trademarks of Sterling Publishing Co., Inc.

Text and illustrations © 2018 William Bee
Paintings © Arty Farty
Arty Farty's agent: Mr. Grimaldi

First Sterling edition published in 2018.
First published in the United Kingdom in 2018 by Pavilion Children's Books, 43 Great Ormond Street, London WC1N 3HZ

All rights reserved. No part of this publication may be reproduced, stored in a retrieval system, or transmitted in any form or by any means (including electronic, mechanical, photocopying, recording, or otherwise) without prior written permission from the publisher.

ISBN 978-1-4549-3293-2

Distributed in Canada by Sterling Publishing
c/o Canadian Manda Group, 664 Annette Street
Toronto, Ontario M6S 2C8, Canada

For information about custom editions, special sales, and premium and corporate purchases, please contact Sterling Special Sales at 800-805-5489 or specialsales@sterlingpublishing.com.

Manufactured in China
Lot #:
10 9 8 7 6 5 4 3 2 1
07/18

sterlingpublishing.com

Here is Arty—busy painting another masterpiece.

He's the Greatest Artist in the World!

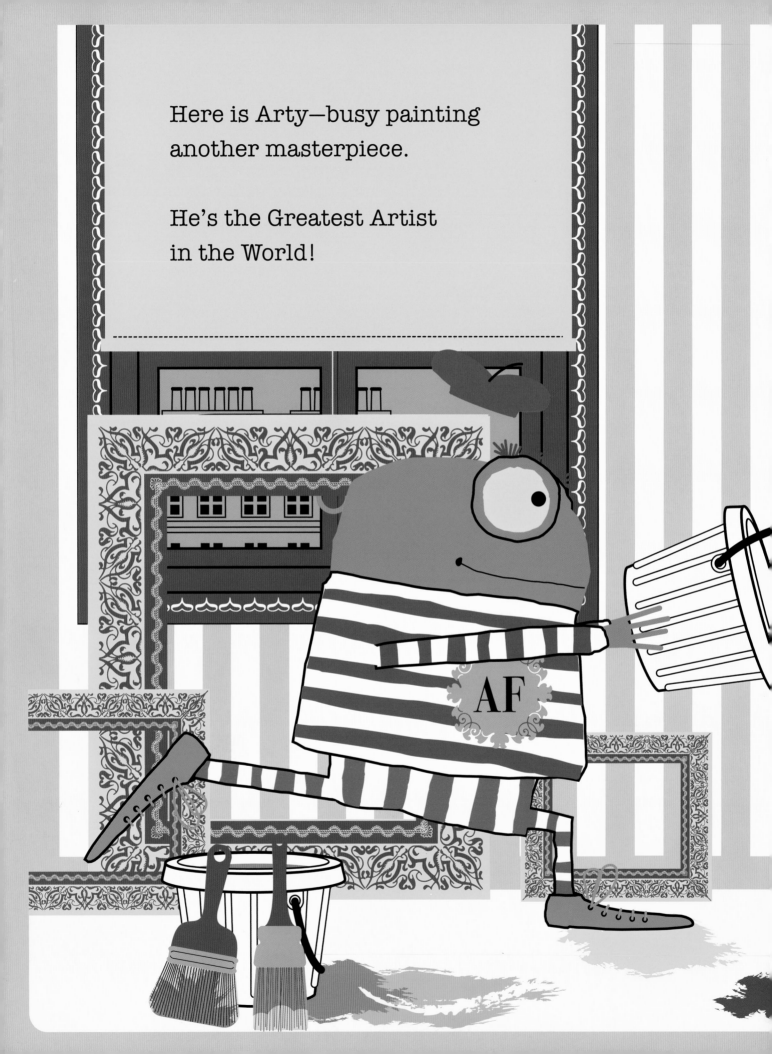

But how did Arty become the
Greatest Artist in the World?

LEFT

RIGHT

BUY ONE GET ONE FREE!

The first thing Arty had to do, to become the Greatest Artist in the World, was to order a pair of snowshoes, a nice warm winter coat, and a very tall stepladder.

| XS | S | M | L | XL |

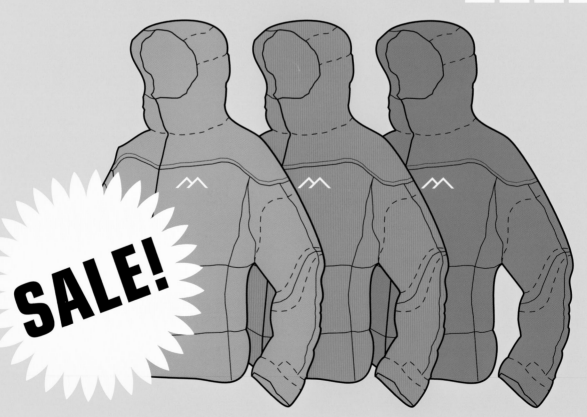

SALE!

Balmoral
H: 8 feet

Windsor
H: 2.5 feet

Sandringham
H: 6.5 feet

Kensington
H: 4 feet

Highgrove
H: 7 feet

EXCLUSIVE STEPLADDER COLLECTION!

The next thing Arty had to do,
to become the Greatest Artist in the World,
was to climb to the top
of the highest mountain in the world—
Mount Everest.

And then,
just to make sure,
Arty climbed to the top
of his stepladder.

And
then
what
did
Arty
do?

He
painted
the
highest
painting
in
the
world!

"And
the
coldest,"
said
Arty.

"After that, I need a couple of weeks lying in bed," thought Arty.

No such luck!
The next thing Arty had to do,
      to become the Greatest Artist in the World,
   was to climb on the wing of
         a supersonic jet.

This is Mr. Grimaldi.
He sells Arty's paintings.

Strapped on very tightly,
Arty painted,

sometimes upside up,
sometimes upside down,
sometimes looping the loop.

It's the *fastest* painting in the world!

After Arty got back down on the ground,
he finally spent a couple of weeks lying in bed.

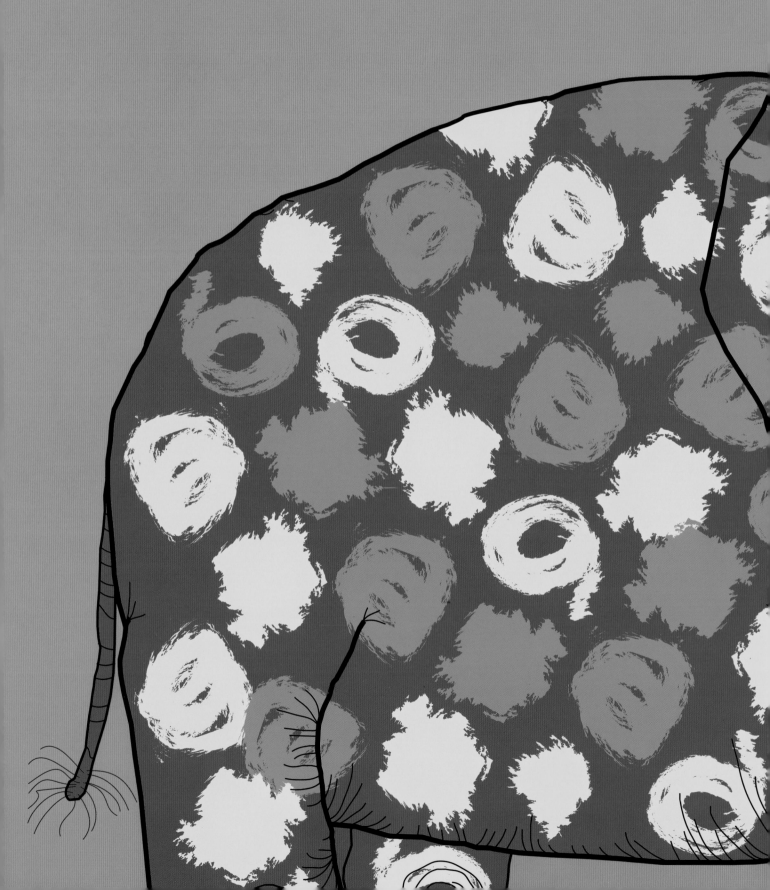

Then he caught up with his friend Tallulah
and painted the *spottiest* painting in the world!

Next!
Arty painted the *lightest*
painting in the world,

which floated away...

the *wettest* painting
in the world,

and high up
on the highest...

of high wires...

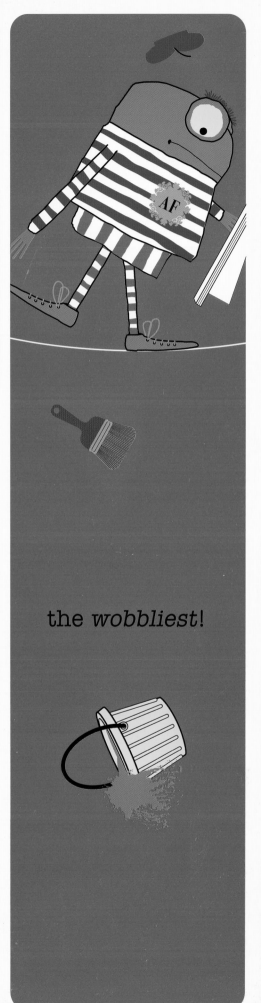

the *wobbliest!*

Then Arty did the next thing he needed to do
to become the Greatest Artist in the World.

He painted as many pictures as he could—all at the same time

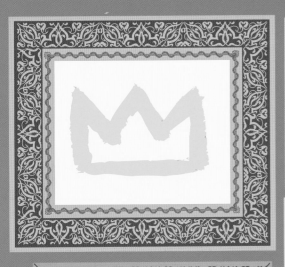

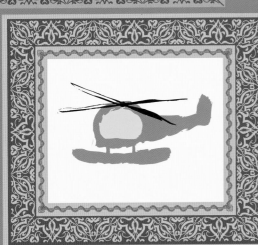

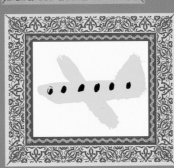

Twenty-four of them—
all at once!

"I am like an artistic
octopus!*" said Arty.

Arty loves to play his great big drum.

"This is definitely the *loudest* painting in the world!" shouted Arty.

And what is this?

"The prettiest painting in the world," said Arty.

The *hairiest* painting in the
world also turned out to be...

"...the *scariest!*" said Arty.

"Now if all that doesn't deserve a couple of weeks lying in bed," thought Arty, "what does?"

"YOU CAN LIE IN BED WHEN YOU ARE THE GREATEST ARTIST IN THE WORLD!" shouted Mr. Grimaldi.

Arty
reluctantly
got out of bed
and climbed
onto a giant
trampoline.

So did
Mr. Grimaldi.

Up they both go,
and down they
both go, and up
they both go,
and down they
both go,

Arty brushing paint onto the picture

whenever he gets anywhere near it.

"This is worse than being strapped to that supersonic jet!" said Arty.

But it's worth it! For the *bounciest*
(and *messiest*) painting in the world.

Arty really does need a nap now,
and so does Mr. Grimaldi.

And *that* is how Arty became...

...the GREATEST Artist in the World!